Wicket Goes Fishing

AN EWOK™ ADVENTURE

by Melinda Luke
illustrated by A. O. Williams

HAPPY HOUSE BOOKS
Random House, Inc.

 Published in the United States by Random House, Inc., New York, and simultaneously in Canada by Random House of Canada Limited, Toronto. ISBN: 0-394-87971-6
Manufactured in the United States of America 1 2 3 4 5 6 7 8 9 0

It was spring in the Ewok village. As the first rays of morning sun filtered through the trees, Wicket bounced out of his hammock. He had the whole day planned—he was going down to the river to try out his new fishing rod for the first time!

"I'll bet I catch more trout than ever today!" he said, and hurried outside to get ready.

Wicket saddled his pet bordok, Baga, packed a big lunch, and strapped his bait and rod to the saddle. "It's just you, me, and the trout today!" he said happily, giving the bordok a little pat. "No Woklings to worry about!" Wicket was really looking forward to spending a day alone in the forest. He was tired of the hustle and bustle of the village, and he was especially tired of Woklings. They always tagged along after him and got in the way. He'd had enough of baby-sitting, too.

Just then Wicket's mother and baby sister, Winda, walked by. "Where are you going, Wicket?" asked his mother.

"I'm going to try out my new fishing rod," said Wicket.

"Why don't you take Winda along?" suggested his mother. "She'd love to go with you."

Wicket groaned. A Wokling—his own baby sister—on his fishing trip? She'd ruin his day for sure! "But, Mama—" Wicket began.

A stern look from his mother told him there was no point in arguing.

"All right, she can come," said Wicket gloomily. "But she'd better be good."

Winda beamed happily and scampered along after her big brother.

"You're too little to walk to the river, Winda," said Wicket. "You'll have to ride Baga." He lifted her into the saddle. "Don't touch *anything*! Understand?"

Winda smiled sweetly and nodded her head.

Wicket scowled as he took the reins and led Baga out of the village. He hadn't planned on walking all the way to the river. And he certainly hadn't planned on taking care of Winda!

The forest was cool and smelled of pine and honeysuckle. As Wicket walked along the path, he thought about the river. It must be teeming with trout. "I sure hope the fish are biting today!" he said.

Just then Winda began to giggle.

"What's so funny, Winda?" called Wicket.

Winda laughed and pointed to the path behind her. A trail of worms was wriggling into the woods. They were coming from Wicket's bait basket!

"My bait!" cried Wicket. "How could you let them get away?"

"You said, 'Don't touch anything!'" said Winda. "So I didn't."

Wicket scowled. "I guess I can catch some more when we get to the river," he said.

Wicket kept walking, and before long he noticed that Winda was being awfully quiet—too quiet! When he looked back, he saw that she was fast asleep, with her head resting on Baga's saddle. "She can't cause trouble while she's sleeping," he thought happily.

Soon they came to a small clearing. "This looks like a good place for a picnic," said Wicket. But when he opened his saddlebags, he found they were empty. Wicket searched frantically through each one for the food he had packed. Fruit, nuts, sandwiches, and juice—everything was gone! Winda had eaten every last mouthful!

"I guess I can eat fish for lunch," he said with a sigh.

Wicket tried to keep his eye on Winda when she woke up from her nap. But then the trail narrowed and he moved ahead to clear the brush from their path. When he returned, he found Winda twirling his new fishing rod around like a baton. *"Put that down!"* he shouted.

Winda let go, and the rod came crashing down. It hit a rock and then fell into a clump of bushes.

Wicket chased after it. He shoved aside the bushes to find the rod in pieces on the ground.

"Bad Wicket!" giggled Winda. "Mama said never to play in poison ivy!"

Wicket looked around him and suddenly began to itch! "That does it!" he shouted angrily. "I've had it with you, Winda. First you let all my bait loose, then you eat my lunch! Now you've broken my brand-new fishing rod, and on top of that I've got poison ivy! I'm sick and tired of this! We're going home!"

Soon they arrived back at their hut.

"Wahhh!" cried Winda, running into her mother's arms. Wicket stomped in behind her and sat by the fireplace. Their mother listened to the whole story and shook her head.

"There, there, Winda," she said. "Wicket didn't mean to hurt your feelings. Did you, Wicket?"

"And I suppose she didn't mean to break my new fishing rod, or eat my lunch, or lose my bait, or *ruin my day*?" he cried.

"That's enough, Wicket," said his mother. "Go over to Logray's hut and see if he has a powder for that rash."

Wicket stomped out the door.

Logray was the old medicine man, and Wicket loved to visit him. "I have just the potion for your poison ivy," said Logray. "It will only take a few minutes to prepare."

While the medicine man worked, Wicket told Logray about his terrible day with Winda and how fed up he was with Woklings. "They follow me everywhere, they get in the way, and they're always breaking things," he wailed.

Logray stopped for a moment and then added an extra ingredient to the powder. He poured the powder into a cup of tea and offered it to Wicket. "This is just what you need!" he said.

Suddenly Wicket's itching was gone. In its place was a warm, drowsy feeling. As Wicket fell into a deep sleep, he thought he heard Logray's voice saying, "Dream, Wicket . . . of lessons learned and forgotten!"

Wicket dreamed of a time long, long ago when he was still a Wokling. He was the youngest in the family. Winda hadn't even been born yet!

It was a misty spring morning. Wicket's big brother Weechee had just gotten a brand-new bow and arrows and was going into the forest for target practice.

Weechee put his bow and arrows into a pouch and strapped them to the saddle of a big, shaggy bordok.

"I'll lead the bordok for you!" offered little Wicket eagerly.

"All right, but be careful!" said Weechee, and they set off into the forest.

Wicket followed his brother up a steep, rocky trail that ran alongside a deep ravine. As the bordok slowly picked his way along the trail, Wicket fell farther and farther behind Weechee.

"Hurry up, you pokey old bordok," Wicket ordered, giving the reins a sharp tug. The bordok stumbled, and as it did Weechee's new arrows slipped out of the pouch and went clattering to the bottom of the ravine!

"Wicket!" shouted Weechee. "I told you to be careful!"

"I know," said Wicket sheepishly. "I'm sorry."

Weechee looked down into the ravine. "I'll never be able to climb down there," he said. "All my arrows are gone—for good!"

"Look, Weechee!" cried Wicket. "You can still use the bow as a slingshot!" He demonstrated by grabbing a rock, setting it against the string, and pulling back. But he pulled too hard. *Ploing!* The string snapped in two!

"I've had enough of you for one day!" cried Weechee angrily. "Go home and leave me alone! You've ruined everything!"

Hurt and confused, little Wicket ran to his Soul Tree. He sat under it all day, thinking about Weechee and the bow and arrows. "I only wanted to help," he sniffled. "It's hard being a Wokling—nobody wants you around, and you're never old enough to do anything by yourself!"

"If I ever have a kid brother or sister, I'll never, ever be mean to them!" he decided.

Suddenly Wicket opened his eyes and looked around. He was in Logray's hut, holding a cup of tea. "I must have fallen asleep . . . I had such a strange dream!"

"Yes?" said Logray with a smile.

"I've got to find Winda!" cried Wicket, leaping out of his seat. He thanked Logray for the healing powder and rushed out the door.

Wicket ran all the way home. Winda was sitting by her mother, having dinner.

"I'm really sorry, Winda," said Wicket. "I wasn't very nice to you today." Winda's face brightened.

"I didn't mean all those things I said to you—I just forgot how hard it is to be the youngest in the family!"

Winda threw her little arms around her big brother and gave him a hug.

Late that night, when everyone had gone to bed, Wicket tiptoed over to Winda's hammock. "Are you still awake, Winda?" whispered Wicket.

"Uh-huh," she mumbled sleepily.

"How would you like to go fishing with me tomorrow?" asked Wicket.